Mr. Fleming's Suicide

A Love Story

Jefffrey Ross

ISBN: 978-1-62420-726-6

Credits

Cover Artist: Designs by Ms G.

From *Song of Myself*
"What do you think has become of the young and old men?
What do you think has become of the women and
children?
They are alive and well somewhere;
The smallest sprouts show there is really no death,
And if ever there was it led forward life, and does not wait
at the end to arrest it,
And ceased the moment life appeared."
Walt Whitman

Foreword by Connie Forrester, MSW, LCSW, BHP
Introduction by Professor Heather Moulton, MA.

Contains Appendix contributions from
Jann M. Contento, PhD (Dr. Quanzo letter)
and
Kim DuBois, MC, LPC (Tom Braddock letter)

Back cover photo, "Despair" by Juliet N. Newton

Reader Discretion is Advised
Dedicated to those who listen more than they talk.
Appendix of Related Documents follows text
Permission Granted for use of the article
"The Siren Song of Vocal Fundamental Frequency for Romantic
Relationships"
by Sarah Weusthoff, Brian R Baucom, & Kurt Hahlweg (2013).

Foreword

Suicide. Just saying the word carries a heavy weight. The mention often seems negative and judgmental. Suicide is perceived as a blame, a stigma, and proclaims you are bad. The word is usually spoken quietly, in hushed tones, and mostly secretively. Many people don't talk about it since suicide, in our society, feels shameful.

Suicides are becoming more popular and are seen as a way to cope or to stop the need to cope. Some suicide events stem from mental illness: Depression, bipolar disorder, or schizophrenia, to name a few. Regardless of the reason for suicide, we as a society typically place a judgment on the victim as being weak.

In my profession, I have worked with clients who have attempted suicide. One of my clients stated simply they were suffering from terminal depression and felt there was no way out.

Regardless of the possible suicide's reason, the primary challenge to treatment is silence. The potential suicide has a lonely existence, and any stigma reduces the chances of their asking for help. They often dare not let anyone in on their plans or reveal they even are considering self-harm. We need to embrace the people who are suffering and help them to not feel alone in their struggle.

I believe we can all help by making it easier to discuss and ask people what they are feeling. If you suspect someone you care for may be considering self-destruction as a coping mechanism, talk to them. You won't make anyone be suicidal by bringing up the situation and asking. By being a go-to person, you may give someone a way out of the tunnel ahead. This book does that: it gives a picture of what one man felt was his destiny. Hopefully, we can together make a small difference and help someone find a different path.

Connie Cornell Forrester, **MSW, LCSW, BHP**
Apache Junction, AZ, July 2022

If you feel suicidal, please dial
988
*The **new** Suicide and Crisis Lifeline
Available 24 hours. Languages: English, Spanish.*

Introduction

I knew I would love Dr. Ross's new story when it began with Walt Whitman. Well, that, and I've known old Ross for a "few" (Hah) years now. We work together at a community college, and I joyfully read his first scathing satire *College Leadership Crisis: The Philip Dolly Affair* shortly after its release in December 2011. I've also seen his band perform at Arizona Moonbucks locations now and again.

In short, I'm a Ross fan, so it is with utter delight I write this introduction.

The story begins with a note. I'm not giving anything away when I say it's a suicide note (hence the title of the novella), but it's so much more. It's insight and quandary, torment and philosophy. For the Ross ficto-verse fans, it has a few Easter eggs to whet our whistles and return us to the space where other Ross fictions have occurred.

Next follows the poetic meat of the text: "the packet," which allows readers to follow Fleming's tragicomic musings through a series of letters and poems. Fleming tells us the purpose of his packet: to (maybe) provide "an explanation for (his) self-destruction."

The reader will have to decide for him-/her-self/themselves if an explanation is truly offered. For me, Ross—through Fleming—captures the maligned present we are living through. That's not to say the story is not timeless; all presents have been maligned, malodorous, or malfeasant.

What Ross does in this book—as he's done in all his books—is hold a mirror to society. Perhaps he'll make you angry; perhaps he'll make you laugh; perhaps he'll promote your books, so there is no way to be angry at the mirror he's holding in front of your face. Perhaps.

Bordering between sarcasm and cynicism, readers will find connection with John Fleming. They/We must take a moment to stop talking and start listening to what his fragments of life tell us. Maybe we can learn something. Maybe.

With greatest gratitude to Dr. Roz: thanks for the stories,

Heather Moulton
Chandler, AZ, July 2022

To Whom it May Concern (if anyone left has concern for old Fleming)

Well, it has come to the final moment. You would not read my novels or articles or poems or love letters. Perhaps you will read this. I, John Fleming, being of sound mind and fairly sound body, have decided to flip the switch on myself… pull the breaker out of the box. Do myself in.

Ok, I'll stop with the tropes. By the time you find this, I will be dead. In an effort to maintain the cleanliness I faithfully admired over the years, I chose a non-violent and non-invasive mechanism to end my life. You will find a hypodermic syringe near my left arm. Let it be entered into the record I injected myself with *10cc of the horse tranquilizer xylazine*. I understand 2cc's would have done it, but I wanted to be sure. I was able to buy a 50cc bottle from a vet supply house for under thirty dollars. I'm sure the purchase was illegal since I am not a veterinarian…. Go ahead. Arrest me. The cause of death, as any autopsy will tell you, was respiratory failure. I was simply in a very deep sleep. I have been tired for some time. The rest will do me good. Yes. A long rest.

To prove my sanity, I am compelled to share a few stats and scholarly articles with you. Please bear with me.

An organization called the <u>Suicide Prevention Resource Center</u> noted in 2020 that suicide-successful men over age 65 used firearms 75% of the time. Fooled you big time. No blood, no mess over here.

Oh sure, I thought about jumping off the Brooklyn Bridge, the Golden Gate Bridge, or the Nanjing Yangtze River Bridge. At one time, I considered climbing up Everest for hurtling over a cliff or making a pilgrimage to Japan's Aokigahara Forest, the suicide forest near Mt. Fuji. Really, I don't like to travel outside of Arizona. Upon further review, the

Japanese forest experience seemed too paranormal for me. So, I ordered me up some horsey drugs. Yeehaw.

No, I did not end my life because of health problems or emotional issues. Oh, my AC1 was a little high. I got Frankenstein-shocked out of Afib a time or two. I remember now, back in 2018 when the PA told me I had Afib, I felt like a broken robot, a clanky old has-been. I did, sadly, begin drinking only non-alcoholic beer. Well, beta blocker medication didn't work, but the high voltage dropped my pulse rate from 115 to 72, for a time

I hadn't been moody or depressed. I think a kind of weariness, or philosophical erosion, or sadness, or loneliness, kind of did me in. Here is the basic explanation. The formula, the algorithm for my current circumstance, goes something like this:

1. Life in the USA has a predictable script.
2. The script seemed increasingly flawed to me.
3. My efforts at succeeding without the script failed.
4. Drizzle in a little everyday loneliness and isolation
= find the syringe and "get-er-done."

I read something by the crazy old guitar-playing potbellied-professor, Ross, about "The Text" (see appendix below), the script we all follow like zombies. His article didn't do me any good, either:

> I have developed a frightening, yet powerful awareness. I now stand, mannequin-like, in the store window of life, grimly watching the Text-driven crowds shuffle down the sidewalk, drifting into the distance, subsiding into the horizon. (Ross, 2009)

Hopefully, my lengthy suicide discussion will provide clues to therapists and "concerned" psychologists about the causes of my demise. I suppose there are many reasons to write death notes. Perhaps suicides have something to reveal or confess. Maybe they sense a need to craft some sort of written addendum to a will. Maybe they want to tell everybody they are sorry for making a mess or causing trouble. Truth be known, I don't care about any of such matters on a personal level. I'm not sorry. I'm only going to miss my dog and the one person I really love. I just don't care what you think. I suppose, if anything, I hope my packet will be instructive. Yes. Fleming the social reformer. Not likely. You will all keep on stumbling along like you have in the past: happy with pizza delivery, streamed TV, $10 cups of coffee, and cruises to Scandinavia. Life has become unbearable for me, but more in a sociological than psychological sense. Not so much personal choice outcomes as much as a perpetual external social beatdown.

I simply have no opportunity to live life my way in this crazy country. My sense of desolation is grotesquely immeasurable. I will write something down about my views on the afterlife later. Maybe. I sure didn't feel any shame about killing myself. I don't give a **** about my legacy. I feel no need for apologies whatsoever. Give me a break. I am going to miss my dog more than you can imagine. The love of my life. My truest, best friend always.

I would be honored, however, if the wise professors and effete scholars would consider my scribbles as a shining example of the emerging *death note* genre. At last, I could be mentioned in the same breath as Shakespeare, Poe, Woolf, Hemingway, Plath, and Homer. Yass.

Just think of the controversial lectures at Yale or Harvard concerning old Fleming!

Certainly, I have read about the many suicide attempts by the rich, the famous, the actors and athletes, who failed to kill themselves, then made a living by later telling their emotional stories to admiring fans. Apparently, failed suicide attempts can be lucrative if you know how to market some kind of new awareness about the joys of living. Knaves. Egad. Fakes. Pretenders. Bums.

If you are reading this, you are safe from any future discussions by Fleming. He is finished. Kaput. No infomercials, movies, or books. No documentary. No guest appearances on insufferable cable news.

I will let you decide what led to the end of Fleming. The compilation of these unmailed, unpublished, and fragmented notes, poems, and letters below will provide evidence and clarity. This small but powerful packet provides an explanation for my self-destruction. Did I hold grudges too long? I was never loved, that's for ******* sure. Was I right all along? Trust me, I had a box filled with all kinds of papers, letters, and scribblings related to this event which I gleefully burned up on my charcoal grill. The curling smoke was amazingly mystical.

I just saved the missives and scraps I thought articulated my views for this paperclipped packet. I did not put them in chronological order. I figure the ones included here show my feelings best. Looks like my bent-for-hell attitude really started to crystalize back in 2017 or so. Surely, the crazy pandemic lockdown of 2020 ultimately "fried" me and amped up my death note scribbling. The last couple of years have been exceedingly brutal on so many levels. I guess the world as I knew it pretty much ended with 2019. For all of us. Gone, and not coming back.

The macros, the micros of my existence became too much. Shouldn't there be comfort and joy at some time of the day? Late at night when the birds stop singing? At sunrise with a hot cup of coffee, snuggled in a blanket, after a good night's sleep? Not for Fleming. Not for a decade or two or three. Neither the days nor nights would leave me alone or let me rest. A kind of wind, unforgiving and brutal, hot, and cold, howled mercilessly inside my head. Laughing sparrows flew in, then out, of my ears, leaving puffy feathers and putrid droppings. I slept with ants and termites. I crawled on my hands and knees, heart palpitating, breathing labored.

I was such an uncomfortable mess. My soul, or what was left of it, begged for mercy 24/7. Something had to stop.

You should know I wrote this "final" note a few weeks in advance of my peaceful "doomsday." The February 2 date is correct for the time of my demise. I dated and printed this page earlier this morning, after some revisions. I had a scary time with verb tensing. Tough to write in past tense when you're still alive. I couldn't find an appropriate,

4

consistent tense or mood. I guess. You will find some incomplete sentences, a few odd grammatical structures. I ran out of time. Literally.

Oh, let's not have a celebration of life for me. If some of you want to get together, get drunk, smoke dope, or look at old pictures, well, I can't stop you. Maybe set up a boombox and play Clapton's "I Can't Stand It." Go ahead. Play my all-time favorites "Creep" or "Breakfast at Tiffany's." Even one of the 90s Prof. Ross recordings like "Heart Justice" or "Spin Reader" would do. Any country western song about broken relationships would work, too. Please, no fund raisers or potlucks. No "sending prayers" emojis for sure. No "hugs." That is the kind of **** which pushed me over the edge. Maybe celebrate my departure with gusto. Please keep my obit simple: birth and death dates. Please, just let it go. I was miserable and lonely in life. Don't pretend otherwise. You didn't like me when I was breathing. Why get emotional now?

So, this would have been my 75th birthday. I was still running, lifting weights. In decent physical shape for a man my age. I think the first 45 years or so were good. I faced many of life's challenges common to Americans. I have lots to say about this. I was married twice. I left the first wife for another woman. The second wife left me for another woman. The image of those two, after telling me they were in love, walking away holding hands and laughing, commenting on my stupidity, well, the moment still troubles me.

A few days later, I was at the grocery store. I was buying potatoes for an evening soup.

I saw three men talking on their phones, waving their arms, anxious, pensive, stymied by events and situations beyond their control. They were cowering, so afraid. Very distraught.

One fellow was receiving instructions from his significant other about what kind of canned tomatoes to buy (diced, sliced, stewed or whole?). The poor man was sweating profusely.

One husband could not find a small size container of parsley flakes. He was afraid of the beating he would take at home.

Another grimaced, holding his Blueberry against his ear, waiting for his wife to answer, knowing full well he forgot the coupon and was now in trouble. The Blueberry kept banging into his head, banging into his head.

At that moment, I was so glad Wife #2 had left me. Gone. I was free from all spousal banter. I loaded the red potatoes into my motorcycle's saddlebag. Satisfied, I rode triumphantly out to the travel trailer.

Back then, I was still drinking real beer. I had a few (only nine or ten). Oh, I felt way better, so much better. Nonetheless, something was troubling me, something was chiseling at the fabric of my well-being. I thought about the frantic guys at the store. Those silly SOBs at the grocery store were probably happy in life, anyway. I was not. I was freaking miserable. This realization may have been the beginning of my final descent, my final downward spiral.

Speaking of beginnings. I don't have any exact recollection of when I decided to end things. I have some memories of standing in my trailer with a coffee cup, in the winter of 2018, simply asking my reflection in the microwave window: "Would this be a good day to get it over with? What if you killed yourself this afternoon?" I know I wasn't suffering from a bad day, or depression, or sickness. I was just initially feeling ready to be done. The self-questioning was matter of fact: not emotional, not teary-eyed, not speculative. The idea of weeping, or seeking help, or telling friends never once entered my mind. None of my struggles, or my decisions, were any of their business. Then or now.

My close friends, many who have preceded me in death, um, most had happy marriages and families. Families who loved them, respected them. I did not. I had a daughter from the first marriage, and no children in the second. My daughter, Minerva, has not spoken to me for several decades. I am certain she will not be sad to see me go. If she ever learns I am done for good. Such is life. Such is death. I suppose I created those "detachment" issues with her myself. I left her mom for a *plein air* painting artist (an awful hook-up which went nowhere, by the way) when Minerva was only nine.

I have nothing to leave my daughter except my trailer, a few guitars, and copies of the books I have written. (You'll find an unlocked fireproof box in my trailer with all kinds of endgame papers and books, signed, ready to go.)

What was I thinking? I missed so many soccer games, tap dance lessons, birthday parties. All of it. Oh. About the artist I mistakenly got involved with. She went crazy too. She ran off with a coffee house musician from Avondale. I heard, finally, they both ended up in alcohol rehab. Served the bee-atch right.

~ * ~

Now, at the very end, I love a dog and an amazing woman. Without reflection or reservation. Totally. I know the dog loves me. Most assuredly I know the woman cannot love me. This is ok. For sure. Good for her.

I hope somebody reads this packet. Who knows? I'm not a celebrity, crazy actor, or cable news talking head, so I probably won't have much of an audience.

~John Fleming

July 4, 2015
John Fleming's Romance Lament

I am John Fleming. I am melting in the Gila Bend desert sun. Gradually.

I was silly, long ago.

I thought those cute girls noticed me.

Oh, I was not the best looking, not at all. I was thin and probably showed signs of inadequate exercise as a child, or impolite behavior, or misplaced small-town narcissism. I owned two or three pairs of jeans and a shirt or two.

I always looked the same, unkempt and erratic.

I was keen on worthless things like mysteries of the chilly Canadian north, blond furniture in old stone houses, pickled eggs, the glorious smell of burning leaves on late October evenings.

I wanted desperately, while sitting on a stack of hay bales, to hold some pretty girl's gloved hand, maybe cuddle near a bonfire with other happy couples. Just laughing, talking, and dreaming. Making plans. Joyfully.

Never happened. They laughed at me. Over and over again.

Of course, the young ladies I knew, well, I suppose I flirted with them, and tried silly games with them, and made some foolish boasts to them.

Well, they moved on to real life and nice homes.

I tried life a couple of times. Possibly three. Didn't work.

Now I live in a cute tiny home.

I see their faces, still beautiful, poised, always kind, etched in my memories.

Etched by acid. They are happy. I am not.

My diet is better now, but I still don't know how to behave. Cash is hard to come by for me.

*I currently live with a **Big, Mean, Virginia Slims-smoking former psycho-therapist** who would like to smash me with her Bare Hands.*

*Some nights she has bad dreams about Van Gogh's gender confusion. Shrieking**, she pummels my face with her fists**, until blood oozes on the pillow, until her frenzy wanes, until the screaming stops.*

Most nights, I wake up at 3 am. Then, I see clearly I never had a chance with life.

Probably too impolite, too silly, too honest.

The world has passed me by. My time is in the past, too. Now the clock will stop. Finally.

I am John Fleming. Yes, I am melting in the Gila Bend desert sun.

~John Fleming

June 28, 2021

Dear Therapists,

I'm sure I caused some big problems for Minerva. Even so, I must tell you. I am not certain she is actually my daughter. My friend, the psychotherapist Dr. Euyan, was hanging around the house a lot back in those days. (BTW, the ******* guy fired me from counseling. See his letter below in appendix.)

Oh well. The sociobiologists will tell you only the mother can be certain a child is actually hers. At least without a TV show DNA test. Yet another area of study I should have left alone.

I had a good career as a high school math teacher for over thirty years. I enjoyed my students and the secondary school environment in general. I think I have a master's degree in math. I know I taught foundations to intro algebra as an adjunct at Copperfield Community College for many years. The president of said middle-ed institution, Philip Dolly, was legitimately crazy. Really nutty.

I was never rich, but my standard of living was fairly good. Until I cashed out in 2012 to buy that 1968 travel trailer/camper with the leaky roof.

~John Fleming

August 29, 2018
Fleming, the Broken Robot

In the old days,
My tube arms and claws were all the robot fashion.
I looked a bit like Bender.
Now, hardly empathetic, or sympathetic, Artificial Intelligence lives in a chip, and sails through clouds, while I struggle with a dimming identity and lonely circuits.
Patina covers dented casings.
My lead acid battery won't hold a charge. I am human enough to despair, and
I dread the terminal reboot.
I am old robot with nothing left to say.
Rusted, broken, past my time.
~John Fleming

September 20, 2020

Dear Dr. Euyan Quanzo,

I just tried your suggested structured teddy bear cuddling therapy. It did not work. I felt sorry for the poor stuffed animal. I began weeping. Profusely. Bad idea. Poor bear. Poor me. All I can do is stare at those lifeless black plastic eyes and feel worse than ever. Why did humanity ever create miserable stuffed animals? Why? Why? I keep buying stuffed bears and lions and penguins, but I do not feel any better. Plus, I sense I am making the poor inanimate creatures uncomfortable. Euyan, who did your learning? Where is your mind? In a bucket of crawdads? Some old bacon rinds?

~John Fleming

September 25, 2021

To My Beloved,

If this were a movie, you would leave your East Coast husband and family to come live with me in the archaic forest. The squirrels, elk, and deer would eat acorns and apples from your hand each morning. I would have a ponytail, sculpted muscles, and always say clever things. I would have the best tattoos in Northern Arizona. A wonderfully sad but uplifting soundtrack would follow us from coffee houses to wine bars.

You might weep, gracefully, because of your wrenching decision to leave the old world behind, but my strong stallion arms would comfort you. The closeups of your tears would hush the cosmos. We would make love on the beach at <u>Mormon Lake</u>. Maybe in beautiful meadows filled with butterflies and wildflowers.

At night, often, we would sit on a romantic log next to a quiet campfire. We might interpret the meaning of meteors, comets, and galaxies in the clear but dark sky, while a piano tinkled in the distance. Our conversations would be intimate, loving, focused.

Wait, there's more:

Suddenly, my books would become best sellers. Filthy rich and famous, we'd sail the Mediterranean Sea with Eric Clapton, Sheryl Crow, and other celebrity musicians. You would enjoy smoking fragrant herbal cigarettes with EC while he listened intently to my acoustic guitar performances. In fact, everyone aboard the four-masted yacht would stop what they were doing to enjoy my music. Feet tapping. Bodies swaying.

In actuality, this isn't a movie. If you are reading this, well, my late-night comedy show is over. This leading man has vanished. Yacht concert cancelled for good. There was no happy conclusion for us, my love.

~John

December 16, 2021

Dear Adventure Motorcycle Touring Friends,

Truth is, I do not have any such friends. I never liked riding with anybody. Too weird for me. The idea of standing in the shade next to parked motorcycles somewhere drinking coffee and talking about the Alaska-Canadian Highway is not remotely interesting to me. I thought about what the audience might be for this part of my "decline" message. I guess people who ride their motorcycles on the dirt or street might be interested. It's too late to change it now.

Anyway, I have enjoyed riding my 250cc dual sport motorcycle, at times, over the years. The single cylinder machine is a bit underpowered for road use but has been more than adequate for desert trails and forest roads here in Arizona. For a while, I considered using the motorcycle as the primary means to kill myself. I had two basic plans. Both would be messy and violent. In the least romantic scenario, Plan A, I could just swerve into oncoming traffic, especially when a large Peterbilt truck was available, and collide head on. That would do it. Not pretty, but fast. I'll come back to Plan A in a minute.

Plan B initially seemed far more fetching to me. I could ride my motorcycle off a cliff, preferably into the Salt River Canyon on US HWY 60, get nicely airborne, then plummet to a possible fireball death hundreds of feet below. Such an idea always intrigued me because it would probably make national news. Perhaps someone would finally recognize my cleverness, my flair. Just possibly a person would accidentally capture some drone footage of the spectacle. There is no shortage of folks flying drones around anywhere. A drone is looking at me through my window as I type this in December 2021. Oops, there it goes. Buzz!

What stopped from Plans A and B? Well, in no ranked order:

1. I didn't want to somehow fail in my primary objective and then be paralyzed or hospitalized for life. I didn't want to fail completely and then be locked up in a mental institution or be required to seek counseling.

2. I didn't want to damage my motorcycle. Why should the unfortunate thing be destroyed on my account? By the way, the machine has a happy new owner as I write this.

3. An innocent bystander or driver might get hurt. Not my intention. Even people obsessed with self-destruction can still maintain concern for others. Who knows? Some non-crazy people out there might actually be happy and fulfilled.

4. The whole idea of planned death-by-motorcycle just appeared too flamboyant or showy to me. Horse tranquilizer seemed the way to go the more I thought about it.

~John Fleming

August 2019
In the Archaic Forest

Sometimes I sleep beneath
Ponderosa pines
In the archaic forest.
Alone at last in a sleeping bag with tears, with broken zippers,
I see a curious moon staring at me, and I wonder where the flaming weeks and months have gone.
Why my memories are remorseful, stained, and grim.
Birds are quiet now. Only a midnight breeze whispers through sleepy, dark trees.
In the cold night air, I gaze through branches. Yes, I want to go Home.
I love the archaic forest. Still, I must go Home soon.
~John Fleming

October 31, 2018

My Dear Dr. Quanzo,

I disagree with your recent diagnosis or conclusion that I suffer from delusional psychosis. Pah. You know full well I have long had an active, an inventive, mind. I especially resent being told I may suffer from Erotomania. What did I say in our sessions which leads you to think I believe another person, especially one of high social status, is in love with me? I have increasing doubts about the value of Gestalt therapy and contextualization. I know you are an MD also—please just prescribe some heavy-duty tranquilizers or medicating drugs for me so I do not suffer, either from the demons that plague me or from your misplaced analysis of my condition. How about some Thorazine, lithium, or Imipramine? You know, the good old-school stuff that works. Please, doc, I cannot be fixed. Please ease my pain. For the Love of God. Please. Please. I can't stand much more.

Sincerely yours and sinking,

~John Fleming

August 5, 2021
John Fleming Near the End

Old Fleming was near the end, now.

He was living in a travel trailer—or at least a camper on a trailer.

Just off the 747 Road near Happy Jack.

His belongings were crammed into sun-beaten blue plastic tubs.

He had a few pots and pans, some LED lanterns, an AM radio, and a sleeping bag.

He was ostensibly free (but still enchained.)

On warm days, he would lean against a pine tree and read books about Gestalt therapy, Freud, and interventions.

At night he thought deeply about his mistakes. He then wished he could shapeshift into a coyote

Or owl. Then vanish into the forest.

John Fleming suddenly became old— too worn out.

Fleming was not sick, but he was very tired.

So many questions had no answers.

His cash was about gone now. A harsh winter was coming.

Fleming had eaten ramen noodles for eighteen days. Empty trail mix bags, beef jerky wrappers, and Thorazine containers littered the camper and damp ground.

Fleming had seen, had heard, enough.

Each evening, the forest wind discretely whispered answers to his questions, but John could not translate the language just yet.

Mysterious answers were stuck somewhere in a gully, or a bird's nest, or beneath broken tree limbs on the forest floor, or in an old grass fire burn scar.

Fleming would stay in the woods until he deciphered the mystery and could go Home.

(He frequently prayed to go Home. He wanted to be Home for good.)

Or until the Arizona Department of Pine Forests told him to move.

He couldn't remember how he got here. He had no plans for where he might go.

(He never understood the purposes behind Mickey Mouse or prom night or the Milky Way, either.)

Fleming was near the end now.

The wind whispered while he patiently stirred pork ramen noodles over a smoky campfire.

~John Fleming

January 1, 2022

My Beloved, my Querida,

I thought and fretted so long before writing this to you. All those emails, all the collegial moments. Holidays, sad events, emojis. The music. Our memes. Surely a year or two of rippled, wavy virtual moments I will cherish at the end. Baring my soul to you is difficult, exceedingly difficult. Even now when I am dead and gone.

(Yes, I got the term "Querida" from *The Addams Family* TV show. However, "Querida" existed before and after Gomez.)

Hard to see what began my connection with you. True, I have been habitually delusional. Not just in your case. The decades of romantic and familial disappointment convinced me, somehow, that fate, or grim Thomas Hardy determinism, had brought us together at some level. Some sort of redemption for me. You, wisely, never saw such a relationship. I have so much to say about this. It is sickeningly complicated. A mess. Part of my attraction to you was because you showed little interest in me, or at least interest of a romantic, improper nature.

Oh, you were polite, caring, and the most special of my friends. Still. Always. You see, I loved you because you are happy. I love the life you live. You are safe from my heart sickness. You are chronically happy. Each of my days has been a challenge. Each of your days is a joy, sprinkled with flowers, animals, friends, and a loving family. My feelings for you cannot be changed. I do not want your feelings about me to change. I have become darkness incarnate.

Do you remember when you attended the mental health conference at Arizona State University-Payson? You flew into Sky Harbor Airport in Phoenix then rented a car to drive up to the afternoon

21

event. I was living near Payson, not far from Happy Jack, in my travel trailer.

Cell phone reception was bad, but we made contact, and arranged a rendezvous. I was so excited.

We visited for an hour or so. Our first, our only physical meeting. We had tacos at the Mas Longhorn Mexican Restaurant. You had a Tecate with lime. I was careful to drink a non-alcoholic beer.

The event was some sort of trigger for me. I never really recovered. When you hugged me and said goodbye, I saw lightning flashes in the bright noon sun. I even smelled lilacs. I was overcome by love, sweet love, flooding and focused. I saw clearly, crystal and framed, the life I had missed. All the music, all the paintings, all the joy. Holding hands on the beach. Enjoying candlelit dinners on Friday evenings.

Some sort of prophecy had been fulfilled for me. The same chilling prophecy of emptiness.

~ The love of your life you never experienced, John Fleming

Fleming misses his Joie: A poem
July 2019

My Joie came to visit me—indirectly.

She came to her conference, purposefully. Still, we found time for chips and salsa, even chicken tacos.

I did not meet her inappropriately.

She does her work. I do mine.

My Joie has the careful womanly walk, blonde hair, and dreamy eyes.

Her wisp of life is normal: love and family, three cats, theme parks, homecoming.

No drama, no agitation, no chicanery.

You can pretend the net has shrunk the world—but not for me.

Time and space overwhelm this aging fellow. Current distances and ancient memories tug at my heart.

The plane has taken my Joie back to her family, back to the natural cosmic dance, the rhythmic patter of life, of love.

My Joie is go-ne.

Can I go-on?

~John Fleming

January 28, 2022

My Beloved,

Of course, I continue to struggle/analyze why I am so attracted to you. Here is something I just realized. I even did a little research today to better understand the issue. I love math, for sure. We only met face-to-face one time, as you know, for lunch in Payson. Our "date" was brief. Your voice immediately captivated me. There was a musical quality, a tonal presence, a melody, in the sound of your words which transfixed me then and even now.

If anything, the sound of your voice, the inflection of your phrasings, made me love you anymore. I further reviewed this matter. Bear with me. I read an article called "The Siren Song of Vocal Fundamental Frequency for Romantic Relationships" by Sarah Weusthoff, Brian R Baucom, & Kurt Hahlweg (2013). They discussed sound frequencies related to the human voice, and a concept called the fundamental frequency ($f \circ$) As a mathematical quantity, fundamental frequency ($f \circ$) refers to the lowest frequency harmonic of the human speech sound wave. According to Weusthoff, Baucom, & Hahlweg,

> During courtship, $f \circ$ is one of the evolutionary most important signals for non-visual gender discrimination (which is important for successful identification of potential mates; Junger et al., 2013), and for judging the attractiveness of a potential spouse (Borkowska and Pawlowski, 2011).

I do not believe we are courting, but the sound of your voice overwhelms me, melts me. What an $f \circ$ you have. I love your voice so much, but I understand you cannot love me. That is ok, that is fine. I just

24

wish I could hear your sweet, loving warble once more. I thought about using one of those phone apps to call you. I just couldn't tap the icon. Too painful, my love.

~John

January 29, 2022

Dear Trout,

    My canine, my dog, my confidant. Beautiful when groomed, still A+ lovable two months later. I am closer to you than anyone. Oh, if I could just be in your mind for five minutes. One of my saddest realizations is that I will not be seeing you anymore. At least in this crummy life. No doubt, you loved me more than any human ever cared for me.

    I wish I had given you more treats. Yes, I should have taken you to the grassy dog park more often. Those dog smells. Dog spit. If I had been born a dog, I believe I would have seen things differently. I wasn't so lucky. The odor, the behaviors, of most humans seems so odd, so contrary to me. All those commercials for body wash, for beard gel. No amount of cologne can cover the self-righteous and pretentious human stink. Why can people not stop vocalizing and commenting? ***WHY?***

    I have read in many places that dogs are angels without wings. Did the Lord God Almighty have a plan when he sent you to me? Surely, you reminded me how to love and be loved. Without cost or games. I wish I could be in your mind for just a few minutes. Just a minute, even.

    What is "dog" spelled backwards? Hmm? Don't forget the capital letter. You have been the greatest blessing in my life.

    I will miss holding your paw and scratching your belly. All of that. Your static-lifted ears. Your shrill bark, your thumping tail. Always glad to see me, always sad to see me go. Oh, if I had only been born a dog. We would be a different kind of friends, but still friends, running, playing, going for walks.

    I know you will be happy with your new family in Winslow. Rick will take you fishing, I hope. Please try to remember me and our morning dental treats.

Forgive me, Trout, for I know what am about to do. Saying goodbye to you is the toughest, for you loved me the most. I love you still. Hope we can meet on the other side of the rainbow someday. Your best friend always. Forever.

~Dad

Genesis 3:19

"By the sweat of your brow you will eat your food until you return to the ground,
since from it you were taken; for dust you are and to dust you will return."

December 7, 2021

To my Remaining Family Members, except Minerva,

I have such mixed feelings about you. Love is not one of those feelings. I have grown increasingly numb about family matters. Probably negative. What a joke. All those dinners and holidays. Lord have mercy. Bad food, bad looking people, bad manners. Windbags. Pretenders. Charlatans who believe a joke fixes everything. God gave us two ears and one mouth. Shouldn't we listen twice as much? Why did you never listen? Talk, speak, talk without listening. Ever.

Nothing in my experience has been even close to the warm, fuzzy greeting card fantasy you all seem to enjoy, or what the goofy TV shows hand us. I have been minimized, criticized, and ridiculed by you. Follow your dreams, you say publicly to your friends and neighbors. But I was vilified for following mine.

Somehow, Fleming followed the wrong path, even though he was reasonably happy in the second half of the 20th century. He did what he wanted to do. Then, you never let him forget what a moron he was for not following your advice. Please don't be emotional when you learn of my end. Way too little way too late. I didn't go to med school or law school. I turned out just fine. At least till recently. BTW. Does it occur to anyone that lawyers and doctors help create litigation and medical issues so they can make even more money? Poor guys. So many lawsuits, blood tests, elective surgeries. My my.

Do we really need 10,000 art history professors in this country? Do any one of those eminent chocolate tobacco pipe-smoking scholars know how to unplug a sink with a powered drain auger, or how to use a TDC gauge to time an old two-stroke motorcycle? I doubt it.

In general, you are a self-centered, narcissistic bunch of takers who apparently continue to function as good citizens in a world that cherishes fraud. I don't blame you for what you are. I can assure you, I won't miss you. I enjoyed my childhood immensely. Adulting hasn't been all that great. Thank heavens, I'll miss Christmas next year.

By the way, I have disdain and contempt for people who inherit money and then behave like they had something to do with their improved standard of living. Your big houses and big trucks bought with someone else's cash. C'mon. Random, I know. Just speaking my piece.

~ Your worn-out and infinitely bitter relative

PS. I have nothing but good to say about my grandparents on both sides. They loved and supported me always. Wonderful people. Too bad their affection for me wasn't passed on to the next generation.

November 29, 2021
To Whom It May Concern… the macros that destroyed me.

So much of American life has pummeled me. I find it so cliché, so predictable, so gruesome. America is an unyielding master with 330 million mind-numbed servants. In America, things are always the opposite of what they seem to be.

I decided to fly into Ohio one Thanksgiving to visit some old friends in Columbus. A happy family. This was an effort to cheer myself up and get away from the psycho-therapist for a while. Maybe my face would even heal. At the airport, I slouched in a vinyl chair in some sort of art deco lounge, bathed in pinkish lavender half-light. I carried only a backpack and flip phone. I then turned on my senses.

Immediately, I could smell twelve-dollar fajitas cooking. The hum, the buzz, of energized travelers provided for noisy, incessant, background muzak.

I was watching the passengers stream by, giddy, effervescent, so happy to see each other.

They were speaking the global corporate dialect. Each mimicked the gestures of soap operas and movies. They were mightily excited about funny television commercials, video games, streamed events.

Yes, they were hurrying home for turkey or eggnog or a fresh controversy. Maybe to more predetermined drama and family unity. I asked myself (quietly), "What is the outcome they wish? What are the things they want?" I knew I would walk home in the blasting heat or trudge in scaly snow rather than be seen driving a scripted big-wheeled Lexus. You are owned by your possessions, my friend. I would rather find succor reading the poetry of broken men and women.

More on travel. You people really ought to read Emerson. I

suppose when you travel you go on a furlough from your own domestic prison. Oh, I know. Everyone travels for the sights, the culture, the food, the history. That is all nutty. Travel is a type of social furniture, another boring script-driven discussion topic, a distraction. At least until you retire. Then, you and your spouse travel so you won't have to stay at home and look at each other as you methodically and happily fatten up. If only, if only, you could avoid the Text. If only you had learned to live during your life. But it is easier to be distracted. It is fun to be a puppet.

Someone admonished me: "John, you should go to London someday. I just got back." I asked, "Would that make me more like you?" Dead silence.

Please, someone release me from this crazy world. Ah, thankfully, the end is something even I can manage.

~John Fleming

January 1, 2013
Happy Couples

Sometimes Fleming wonders how
The happy, loving world of couples just slipped by him.
Space and time filled with lovers keen on each other
Enjoying restaurants, cruises, resorts, romance.
Nah, not Fleming's experience.
Planning some kind of future, giving presents, finding moments
with someone special?
Nope, just the whistling pines and a dog for Fleming's friends
now.
Simple support, simple talk, simple voyages together.
Well, he is 66, and pretty rough around the edges. A new romance
is unlikely.
Sometimes Fleming sips on a good cold beer
Hunkered down in his travel trailer, snow or sleet pelting its metal
sides.
He realizes life hasn't been so bad.
There's been no one to nag him, no complaining, no games.
Just lots of time, and speculation.
Sometimes Fleming wonders how
The happy, loving world of couples just slipped by him.
He heard all the stories: holding hands in Tampa Bay, jetting off
to Salem, loving on the Bridge of Sighs, celebrating anniversaries with
roses, big dinners, and those Facebook pledges: Love of my life, best
friend, soul mate girl of my dreams, my love. All that everywhere and
incessantly.
Then, he turns on a night light, rolls over, pulls a stocking cap over

his yellow, hairy, wrinkled, scabby ears. Old Fleming goes to sleep content. Nearby, his dog snores peacefully under the covers.

The next day, the trailer, the trees, and the feelings are still the same.

~John Fleming, a solitary dude who enjoys his quiet life most days.

Feb 2, 2020

Dear Relationship Coaches, Counselors, Advisors,

Boy, you are an interesting bunch. Are you all *wizards?* Wave your wands and effect change. How weird. See you in St Louie.

I read somewhere that a delusion is a mental issue, some kind of false obsession. I also read that an illusion is a simple blurring of reality.

I am here to tell you they are more closely related than what you think. Human romantic relationships, at least the successful ones, are not based on physical attraction, trust, communications, support, values, family life, or any of that calculated rationalist nonsense we hear about daily. Barf.

Relationships succeed when couples buy into the same delusion/illusion and nurture a wonderful fake world together. They enjoy the delusion. It is magnified and strengthened in their functioning dyad. Doesn't matter what constitutes the delusion. Big Careers. Children. Bumper stickers. Crime. Living in the trailer park. Lifting weights. Authoring books. Flipping houses. Playing video games together. Getting drunk together. Dirt bikes. Canasta. Monday Night Football. Going bowling. Shooting rhinos together. Watching DYI shows together. Getting tribal art tattoos together. Riding big V-twins and wearing matching bandanas together. Remodeling together. Cooking. College football. Wine tasting parties. Gardening. Cats or dogs. The list is infinite. They stay together because they share the same delusions/illusions at all costs. Happy lovers are always stuck in some kind of a reciprocating energy feed that keeps them going.

Better to be deluded than face the truth. That's why theme parks, movies, sitcoms, and romantic turmoil on television are all so successful.

No one wants to face reality.

Wait just a moment. Fleming is a balanced, loving, thinker. I am a fair man, for sure. I keep an open mind and heart.

Let's quickly discuss and assesses reality and romance. If coupling was actually grounded in reality, outside of the biological reality-based species demand for procreation, there would be no relationships. Successful couples share delusions. Of course, they may find the illusion of romance appealing (flowers, Valentine's Day, couple photos). But if they don't buy into each other's bizarre fixations, well, their days of happiness are over. Quickly.

In old Fleming's always-accurate opinion, the relationships that work are based on worshipped fraud. Not reality. I'm grounded in a very harsh reality you cannot confront. Adios.

~John Fleming, deluded realist

December 24, 2021

Dear Mental Health People,

I have much to say to you also, but not much you will want to hear. I've often thought misfits go into counseling or therapy because they themselves need help. Maybe listening to other people's problems serves as a distraction or a displacement activity. Most therapists seem quite odd to me. Those same old words keep popping up: boundaries, intervention, voices, delusion, therapy, expectations, issues, disorders, depression, bipolar disorder, therapy, schizophrenia.

Ugh. Groan. On and on without resolution. Do you therapists enjoy having all that stuff inside your own head every freaking day?

I was prescribed Wellbutrin, Cymbalta, and Duloxetine a time or two. Nothing. Now I'd need a bushel basket of those pills before I'd go see a therapist again. What a joke.

My suspicion is that those counselors and such people fill a slot for the great pharmaceutical-mental illness-social engineering complex. Clinics and physicians can check off another box, and they all make lots of money. Everybody wins, except the patient. All those tests and follow-up tests. Nothing changes. People live. People die. Oh, a few poor slobs are maintained for a year or two. Then, they check out of therapy or check out of life. Talk, talk, talk.

Here's an idea. Stop trying to prevent suicides. Why not encourage them? I think people such as myself who really do kill themselves are going to pull the trigger or take the pills no matter how much therapy they receive. Counselors and psychiatrists, all those meddlers, only succeed with pretend suicide people. Meanwhile, the mental health "experts" maintain their professional status, careers, and fat-cat incomes.

Maybe you counselors could all put your energy into working with the families and friends left behind. Simply tell them the truth, give them the facts. Maybe suicide "victims" hang it up because family and so-called friends are lousy people to be around. What if family, friends, or lovers are the real problem? Can't touch that idea, can you smart guys?

Oh. I have heard it over and over: "Suicides cause so much pain for the family left behind." That argument seems ultimately selfish or narcissistic to me. Another way for society to blame or find fault with suicides. Why do you always think of yourselves first? No one listens.

Look. Some people are better off out of the picture. They have seen too much, or heard too much, or realized their crummy lives aren't going to change. You don't need to lay any guilt on the survivors, but please tell them the truth. Stop with the thoughts, prayers, and angel emojis. The candles, pictures, and flower memorials on the sidewalk. Some of us really did have ****** lives. We were happy to go.

By the way. If you are Pro-Choice or Pro-Life on abortion, don't give me any advice on suicide. My body, my choice. My heartbeat. Don't like my logic? I've lived my own precious life. No, I didn't like it. Stop sticking your nose into personal business. Why do you do-gooders, communitarians, and social activists always think you know what is best for everybody? What is your theoretical framework? Arrogance? Artifice? Justice? For whom? Your own sense of misery you desperately need to project onto others? What a better world this would if you could stop acting up.

Ok, just think of my auto-erasure as social euthanasia if it makes you feel better.

Speaking of euthanasia, I'm sure there are instances when clinically acceptable termination, or euthanasia, seems quite appropriate to you. Why not? Sick people are not coming back from a terminal illness. Why should they suffer? Doctor-assisted suicide is becoming more acceptable every day.

I must tell you, life as I have lived it is a painful terminal illness.

Surely many share the Fleming perspective.

Please don't send me the National Suicide <u>Prevention Lifeline</u> phone number, either. Too late. Thank heavens.

Notice much of therapy is related to talking? You might want to rethink your methods. There is way too much talk—not enough action.

~John Fleming

PS Certain words and phrases, part of the daily American psycho-babble, also helped drive me over the edge. The following is a quick list of *overused* terms and phrases I'm sure you will recognize. Think about it. What do they even mean? Listen up! My word selections have no right-wing or left-wing bias. What a joke. My favorite wing is on a chicken or in a song by Jimi Hendrix. You all waste so much time on politics and politicians. How in the world can you believe any politician will "fight for you"?

C'mon. Get a life. Stop wasting so much time. Wait, I know. Most of you have successful careers because nothing is ever finished.

See my list of painful phrases and words below:

(Not in ranked order)
Partner (with)
Hero
Foundation
Core Values
Stand (with)
(Insert word or phrase) strong
Streaming
Inclusion
Identify as
Ciabatta
Circle back
Reach out
Be like

Erectile Dysfunction (Does every man in the country suffer from ED?)

Craft Beer

Top of mind

I got my vaccine

Renew your windows

Camp Lejeune

Battleground states

GOAT

Medicare Part C (and all the *crazy* old has-been celebrities that promote it!)

Podcast

Climate Change

Income equality

Threat to our democracy

Xander

Carbon Footprint

EV

Fascist

Voter Fraud

Supply Chain

Diversity

Conservative

Liberal

LOL

Left

Right

Cruise

Abortion

Road trip

LMFAO

Pray for (insert)

COVID (and all its tiresome variants)

Got your back
Physicality
Global
Bucket List
Solar (insert whatever)
Celebrate (insert whatever)
Border (insert whatever)
Recognize (insert whatever)
National (insert whatever) Day
Follow the science (Hah. Check out those weather forecasts in Arizona!)
Stimulus
Transparency
Team (insert whatever)
Prayers
Hugs
Health care provider
Financial planner
Last chance
Action required
Action plan
Crypto
Shout out
Peeps
Epic
Icon
Impeach
BFF
Showing love
Insurrection
Foundation
Build
Fiduciary

Killing it
Fight for you (us, Americans)
Retirement planning
Husband and wife law team
Fur baby
Donate
Vintage
Fake news
Gender
Influencer
Show some love
Staycation
(Any and every pharmaceutical advertised on TV with 500 disclaimer statements and happy actors who have apparently overcome their itchy medical condition…)
Playcation
Y'all
Culinary (insert word or phrase)
Fossil fuel
Tail pipe Emissions
Pandemic
Elon Musk
Warren Buffet
Any politician since George Washington
Stimulus
Dream destination
Date night
Play date
Career ladder
Rock star
Any and every personalized license plate message
Bundle
Excellence

Physicality
Hybrid
My love
Happy dance
Well played
Gaslighting
How I (we) roll
No worries
Let's do this
Bucket list
Any personalized message on a door mat
Highest level
Next level
High level
Sports book

Recent "drop offs" from list but still annoying
Feedback loop
Shout out
Love of my Life
Paperclipping
Karaoke
Mission statement
Thought leader
Home theatre
Global Warming
Hybrid
The Swamp
Feminine hygiene
Excellence (really an oxymoron!)
Ashley
Jordan
Justin

Logan

A+

Green

Classic rock **(how many times do we have to hear those songs?)**

Wait there's more

Super star

Strategic plan

Robust

Awesome

Flip

ETF

Absolutely

Get real

Alternative lifestyle

Having said that...

Game changer

No brainer

Digital divide

Discount fees

American dream

Broadcast excellence

An honest living

Social media

Ok, so I may have repeated myself in that list a time or two. I probably left out fifty words. So what? I have to hear so many crazy words 10,000 times a day. I got tired of listing them. And you probably wore out reading the list. Are there no original thinkers left? Are you all parrots? Squawk. Squawk. Put on a suit and make a video. Go live on social media. Squawk. Talk. Squawk. Be an influencer\ thought leader.

Run from such people as fast as you can, my depressed and troubled brothers and sisters.

BTW (also wearing). Has it occurred to you yet no one in this goofy country wants resolution to anything? You want to argue, commentate, advise, coach, prescribe, or medicate, or litigate. The truth, though, is you never want to fix or resolve anything. There's no future in movement or resolution. What if therapy really worked? What if we found cures to diseases? Reformed the tax system?

    ~John Fleming

April 2, 2021

Dear Sports Crazies,

Some will question my sanity because I killed myself. Let us see who is really nuts. You know you all are. You talk about sports all day, you listen to the six million bizarre people on the radio and TV who talk about sports all day, you spend hundreds of dollars on tickets to see grown men play kids' games, and you support their 200 million dollar a year salaries while complaining about your own miserable job. See anything even remotely bizarre in all that? What about "income equality," "fight for 15," and all such other economic nonsense?

Here's an idea. Let's make those pro sports contracts really incentive-based. So, some famous point guard in the NBA makes 50 million a year. Let's lock in some "win" incentives to benefit the fan. How about a refund on ticket prices based on wins? So, if "Mack the Strife" (they all have goofy nicknames, don't they?) and his team only win 50% of their games, 50% of their salaries goes back to the ticket purchasers. Old "Mack" would only get 25 million. My idea will never be implemented because it is too simple. How do you like me now? Too bad I'm gone. I have lots of great ideas.

~John Fleming, original thinker

November 7, 2021
The Final Rejection

Fleming sat at a bar in Prescott,
Thanksgiving Eve,
Staring at himself in the mirror
Considering an age-old problem.
The solutions all seemed inadequate.
His loneliness was killing him
Once slowly, now accelerating.
Bad memories and awful dreams filled his nights,
while romantic delusions dominated the daylight
He couldn't tell her how he felt.
Better to suffer with faint hope
Than suffer the final rejection
Or was it?
Then his thoughts turned to the many guns he owned, and the
ammo resting in camo-colored tins at home. Sadly, he just
couldn't pull the trigger. Yet.
~John Fleming

July 5, 2020

Dear Landscapers and Food Home Delivery Drivers,

All the noise is driving me crazy. Blowers, mowers, weed eaters, chain saws, mulchers. Don't you find it ironic or odd? People have lawns and trees to create an illusion of peace and calm while you destroy serenity with your cacophony and odors. You are everywhere in the neighborhoods around the clock: making noise, blocking streets, dropping limbs on the freeways, jamming up the gas stations. All for a completely unnecessary industry.

As you well know, most Americans would rather go to the buffet than cut their own grass. You can take that image to the bank. Speaking of buffets or late-night dinner or snacks. Be careful when you cross the street. You are apt to be run over by a food delivery car.

Yes, food delivery cars and landscaper trucks are fighting for parking spaces everywhere. My, my.

~Tired of noise and traffic, yours truly, the nearly-deaf John Fleming

January 22, 2014

Dear Chefs, Cooks, Eaters, and Snackers,

Here's another societal macro which made my life miserable. Food. Americans have the strangest fascination with food. Don't even try to argue with me. Comfort. Calories, Chocolate. Roasted. Drizzled. Smoked. Fried. Grilled. You think I'm crazy for killing myself, but millions are fat, diabetic, and heading to an early death because they eat too ******* much. Constantly. Stay off my case because I want out of here quickly and without a fat belly.

Fast food. Cooking shows. Snacks. Burritos. Tacos. Sushi. Designer cookies. Buffet. Carry out. Delivery, Dine in. Ugh.

Every department meeting you attend has food now. Lots of it. Finger foods of every design, beanie weenies, quiche, deviled eggs, spinach dip. Endless chips and salsa, brownies, shortbread cookies, chicken wings, chilled shrimp, alfalfa-based spreads, pâté, rye crackers…. So many potlucks, baby shower bake fests, concerns about the donuts still left in the Boss's, Dean's, or Principal's office.

In the 21st century, every event is an excuse for a big meal. Every promotion, demotion, phone call from a telemarketer, successful trip to the gas pump, sunrise, or sunset—each has become a special event which begs, even necessitates, a fusillade of food from the local eatery.

Criminy. There is more. You are not even safe in your domicile.

Chances are good, when you answer the doorbell, cheerful kids (Boy Scouts, Little Leaguers, eager students from the local elementary school) or some bizarre vote-seeking charity groups, are selling cookie dough, pizzas, pretzels, or coupon books shouting discounts at restaurants, eateries, and bistros. "What? Only $22 for a bag of pretzels?

No Problem."

Or "Buy 20 entrees and get one free. Such a deal."

Whew. I need a break. Just start naming, Walt Whitman style, any food words floating through your hunger-wracked Mind. The list is infinite:

Pizza, pasta, pork, provolone.

Cake, caramel, calzones, mutton.

Goose, potatoes, bell peppers, squid, lobster, asparagus, corn-on-the-cob.

Enchiladas, salsa, halibut, liver and onions, runzas,

Leg of lamb, head of pig, brisket, steaks, chops, tenderloin, shark,

Cream sauce, red sauce, cheese sauce, white sauce, Alfredo sauce, soy sauce, hot fudge sundaes, honey ham, BLT.

Gravy, pie, egg noodles, yams, mashed potatoes, olives, antipasto, bacon bits,

White beans, pork and beans, frijoles, quesadillas, green beans,

Aussie chicken, pickled beets.

Crunchy, sweet, sour, gamey, vinaigrette, sea-salt, cayenne pepper.

Kraut, eggs, bacon, pancakes, omelet, sausage links, bologna ring,

Turkey, stuffing, dressing, gizzards, apple pie, oysters.

Shortbread, wheat bread, French bread.

Chicken wrap, turkey wrap, Swiss cheese, skillet dinner.

My, my. Sure is good. Hm-hmm. Pat your belly and loosen up the ol' belt a notch or two. Find your walker so you can head to the buffet. Waddle up the steps and pass gas. Blood pressure a little high? Sodium level up? Don't forget the insulin on your way to the donut shop.

I am so tired of hearing about pot roasts and prime rib. Really. Oh. Buy some berberine at the health foods store. It might help keep your blood sugar level in check.

Nothing I say will stop you from going back for thirds.

Anorexia? Bulimia? How about 1/3 of American adults in this goofy country are obese? Look in a 1970 high school yearbook. You'll see maybe two overweight kids. In 2022, every high school home room is eating quiche and drinking $8 lattes during first hour. A steady stream of app-driven food deliveries clogs up the parking lot. Don't mock me. Don't knock me.

How many obese people do you see in 50s, 60s, 70s, 80s TV shows?

Leave me alone. One good thing about being dead is that I won't have to smell burnt food on grills smoking away everywhere in the neighborhood. I think I will miss beer a little bit, though. How about the one angry master chef who curses everybody? A hero of the people. Rich and famous. I'll bet he talks more than he listens, too.

~John Fleming

August 28, 2021

To The Therapists,

Funny how I don't want to hear you talk anymore, but I hope you read this. I want you to listen. LISTEN.

Here is a significant micro/macro clash pushing me closer to the end. This is something old Fleming assesses daily. Perhaps hourly. The notion is difficult to articulate. I will try. Now.

I am a creative person. At least in my opinion. I am a thinking person. I am self-reliant in an Emersonian sense. I have been to college where I ostensibly studied the collective wisdom of past learned people. Put all that in your Gestalt blender, then reflect a little.

I am rubbed raw, antagonized, beaten, and vilified by the constant interest in entertainment. I really don't give a rat's a** about movies, what basketball players think about China, recorded music, or the great books. I have my own life. I have authored my own articles. I cannot become giddy over some old guys who played with the Grateful Dudes or the Beach Bombs or whatever because I was alive back when they were AM radio stars in the 1960s. Such an interest in what other people do seems corrosive or nonproductive to me. I am a fan of myself. How much of other people's **** do you want in your head?

I am convinced nostalgia is ultimately poisonous, completely noxious. Trust me, history is a wicked stepmother who abuses the present because she is never happy, never fulfilled.

Who were these people that decided *Moby Dick* and *The Great Gatsby* are valuable literary expressions? Take a step back. They are really weird stories. An angry whale and a womanizer. Hah. Spare me. I'd rather read a debate on emics and etics. The American experience framed or reframed? Make lots of money and act up or else you are a loser. Things are never what they seem to be in America. In fact, they are typically the opposite of what is presented to us. You are fooling yourself if you believe the "classics" of American literature tell us anything about the American character. To understand why we're so crazy, best to read de Tocqueville's 1835 *Democracy in America*.

(BTW….my favorite books are *No More Poodle Skirts* by Genene Valleau, *Cold* by Courtney Rene, *Alone in a New World* by Sherry Derr-Wille, any *Graveyard* book by Heather Moulton, and *Loving Leslie* by Christine Young. These books represent real American literature without forced symbolism and decadent Puritan undertones. The "traditional American canon" best be shot out of a cannon! We have far too many PhD's in literature in this country. Reading should be fun.)

Let's get closer to my point. Tattoos. I am not going to be a billboard for someone else's artwork. Oh, you can boast about how you designed the tattoo, or picked the colors, or won an award. So what? If you don't do the tattooing, scratch your skin with ink and pen, so what?

Oh, BTW. I don't want to hear anything about suicide prevention and semicolon tattoos. Way too literary. Solidarity? Pause in life? Potential suicide? Once again, mumbling interpretation. Talk. Talk. Talk. So boring. Just Google semicolon tattoo if you don't believe me.

You are happy you have seen Elton John four times in concert. You had front row seats each time? So what? Learn to play the piano yourself.

Wait. If you enjoy spending $100 a ticket on old hard-of-hearing musical acts, that's your business. And certainly, get all the tattoos you want. Sure, watch old black and white movies all day on $150 a month cable TV. Laugh at crazy Benjamin Braddock when he acts up with a married woman in *The Graduate*. Go ahead and cheer the comic genius Woody Allen in some black and white film. Have at it. Giggle, slobber, and eat some more. It's a free country. That's not the problem. Here's the problem. That's all you got. That's it. Dissent or discussion of nonconformity, any behavior manifesting real individuality, well, all real creativity is mocked and ostracized. Alternative philosophical or behavioral views are never permitted. Your educated, or non-educated, minds are simply RAM for current events, politics, tired, remixed pop culture. How many holidays and sales events do we really need? What an abject mess you have created with entertainment and cable news. You are born, follow the script, then die. Case closed. So many roaches without a clue.

Perhaps the mentally ill are actually the sane ones. And this. Could it be those poor souls on the autism spectrum are actually further ahead in human evolution? More advanced? Hmm? How 'bout them Aspies?

Does art imitate life, or does life imitate art? Neither possibility is appealing, now is it? Not if you accept the Fleming View. Hear me now, you aesthetes.

I am not misanthropic or crazy. I just relish a sanctity of self which is increasingly difficult to maintain because of the constant noise and cultural nonsense emphasized in American life. "Is that all you got? Is that all you got?" Yes, and it is killing me as certainly as any bullet to the head. The algorithm is as relentless and as deadly as the buffet line. Just quicker.

~John Fleming

January 10, 2020

My Beloved,

Do you remember when you sent flowers to me? You were expressing your concern when I was enduring an incredibly sad time, a bleak life episode. You sent those flowers to me with a good heart, with propriety and integrity. You are a professional woman with dignity. The presentation, the fragrance, walking in beauty. <u>Hozho</u>. Harmonious. True aesthetic pleasure.

I was an old man even then. My heart was touched in a manner I cannot explain. I knew why you sent the flowers, and I loved you for it. I was not delusional. There was nothing romantic or pretend or pretentious in your benevolent gesture. Again, I was overwhelmed by emotions I cannot explain. You have such an effect on me daily. I felt like a participant in a loving relationship during a time of sorrow, for perhaps the first time ever. Oh, why did I learn to love so late? Why did unrequited joy abuse me in the final years?

Sometimes, late at night, or early in the morning, I crawl out of a fitful sleep and hope to see you in the candlelit room, sitting in a chair reading, drinking hot chocolate, and enjoying a slice of toast or a warm cinnamon bun. For a moment, I can sense peace, love, a future.

Then, I cry out. In the cold darkness, I cry out your name. Sadly, you do not answer. I am so alone, so miserable. If you read this, I am quickly becoming only a memory.

Now, the time to blow out my own flickering candle is approaching. Please know I loved you with a purity, a sanctified joy, which will live on. You have sustained me these past few months. You made my crummy life almost bearable. I will find peace. I hope. I love you so much, with both joy and pain, by the second, by the minute, by the hour.

~I love you so much but understand you cannot love me
~your Fleming

Nov 4, 2020

Dear Politicians,

Please stop. Just desist. I can't believe anything you charlatans say. Stop sending out all the political stuff in the mail. What a mess. It makes me sick. So many frauds, so many losers. All those speeches on TV. One defaming, tacky, television commercial after another. Does election season ever end? Apparently not in this country. Better than white bread!

If you look at the definition of a politician in the dictionary, you will see a picture of a bag filled with wind. How can any of you "voters" believe in or support anyone who runs for office? They are all fighting for you, looking out for you. Oh, come on. What a quagmire.

Every political ad the candidates mailed out put another nail in my emotional coffin.

Nothing ever gets done because politicians and bureaucrats thrive on the stasis, indecision, and infighting. There must be some genetic disease creating American politicians. Thankfully I am done voting. Garr.

~John Fleming, former voter

January 4, 2022

Dear Pastor Forest,

When you read this, you will know I have crossed over to the other side. I suppose there will be some debate about where my soul ended up. I was a rabid Transcendentalist (in the 19th century American sense) most of my adult life, but I also believed firmly the Nazarene was indeed resurrected and was the Son of the Almighty. I felt "right with God." Significantly, all during my life, I could not have my beliefs codified or shackled by some formal church or polemic system or televangelist. I hope C.S. Lewis was right.

You knew me well—I do not need to explain myself to you. I think our views about the "spiritual" ramifications of suicide are quite similar. We did not believe, like Dante and other medieval minds, that suicide is utter violence against God and deserves eternal punishment in the Seventh Circle of Hell. For example, in the 1320 poem *The Divine Comedy*, miserable suicides transform into gnarled thorny bushes and trees. Harpies then tear them apart throughout eternity. Such a nice, peaceful, poetic image. Ho! Ho!

You told me once many of your preacher friends, back in the day, would stand at the pulpit and voice their opinions about suicide. They promoted a common theme: "Too bad those people had to suffer in suicide, cause trouble for their families, then burn in hell eternally because of their decision to kill themselves, to sin against God." Well, I don't know. I suppose the passages I've read in the Bible provide some clues about what The **Almighty** really thinks:

> "God saved you by his grace when you believed. And you can't take credit for this; it is a gift from God. Salvation is not a

reward for the good things we have done, so none of us can boast about it" (Ephesians 2:8-9). And, "Only God knows what is in a person's heart" (Psalm 139), and what their intentions are.

Of course, Augustine (354-430), in his book *City of God*, preached vehemently that self-murder goes against God. I cannot believe this line of reasoning to be true. Love and Grace shout to me that old Augustine's message is faulty. God will understand what I have done. He won't punish me, I'm sure. I'm a good guy, basically. Unhappy, but a good guy. I'm just trusting Grace, anyway. The H*** with the rest of you. Especially the billionaire televangelists.

~John Fleming, penitent

Feb 10, 2017
Fleming Comes Home

Fleming comes Home from his weekly shopping spree at the Two Dollar store.

Numb from the northern Arizona cold, he leans his '87 Sportster on its jiffy stand.

The old man struggles to get a crinkled key into the front door (numb fingers, you know).

He is living in an older travel trailer now, somewhere north of Happy Jack.

Bad marriages, bad health, bad moods, and disappointment have cleaned him out.

He doesn't notice scrolling marquees, billboards, or television.

Pop culture is just so much debris to Fleming: dust bunnies, roadkill, plastic bottles in the recycling bin.

Our World has beaten him badly: perhaps his fault, perhaps not.

He can no longer work but pays his bills.

Fleming sees the end of his days on the near horizon.

John treats himself to smoked oysters and a six pack of good cold non-alcoholic beer each Friday night.

He cannot sleep. He is crushed by solitude and sorrow.

The World has beaten him badly: perhaps his fault, perhaps not.

~ * ~

He has no photographs in his place, no phones, nor any past or future.

Just the present.

His memories focus and refocus on those who have ridiculed him mercilessly.

None of the past is good.

He once read and reflected quietly.

Now he cradles his balding, scaly head in gnarly hands, and weeps hourly.

He cannot sleep, he cannot rest.

He cannot smile or dream.

He is too different, too odd.

No one kissed his forehead, or held his hand, or brought him cookies.

You see, Fleming took the sage advice to be an individual: "Never Conform. Be yourself. Do what you want to do. Just Be Happy."

Of course, the World has beaten him for it.

~John Fleming

August 9, 2021

Dear Therapists,

I need to clarify my position on career choices and social issues. It's not just lawyers, doctors, landscapers, insurance companies, administrators, bureaucrats, psychotherapists, and politicians who have caused so much trouble for me. It's pretty much everybody. Yes. Teachers, cashiers, salesmen, journalists, professors, carpenters, fiduciaries, weather girls, attendants, pool boys, technicians, scientists, drivers, servers, superhero wannabees, cannabis clerks, groomers, guys at the smoke shop, programmers, accountants, firefighters, mechanics. All of them and more. Here's why None of you can do your work, get anything done, without making speeches. I don't want a message or TV commercial. I just want the job done. Whatever it might be. I don't want your opinion. Stop telling me you understand my values and goals. You don't have a clue about me. For the Love of God, stop trying to get more of my social security check. It never ends. So, I am going to end it myself. Any time now. Good riddance to all of you. Vaya con Dios.

~John Fleming

February 1, 2022

My Dear Dr. Euyan Quanzo,

    Yes, it is fitting my last scheduled "death note" be sent to you, my former therapist and friend. I am writing to give you final notice of my condition. I feel quite hollow today, quite still. I am an empty, smelly gallon pickle jar. The din of life, the constant talk which has disturbed me mightily over the years, seems to have finally abated. I have not found peace. I have found pause, a stillness, a quiet. Not peace. That is a day or two away.

    My rants and complaints are over now. All pointless and meaningless in the big cosmic picture. I've kicked out my jams, said it all, and actually said nothing. No one has ever cared what I had to say, unless it was part of the Mega Script they understood.

    Emotions, as you well know Dr. Q, are double-edged—both pleasing and damaging.

    Listen doc, I'm not sure what was worse—being lonely all through my 75 years or having to put up with the constant lousy drama of American life. My dog loves me and always will… the best friend, the best companion I ever had. I wasted so much time on frustrating human relationships. So much time.

    All those happy couples and families. Well, could be it was my fault. I'm just too different. Maybe I really am crazy (like one of your counselor friends discretely whispered to you at a group therapy session years ago. Nice.). Certainly, I was never able to value the detritus of day-to-day living. You all get so excited about things you can't wait to get rid of a year or two later. Beats me. Stuff is not so much my problem, anymore. At least not much longer.

I've been circling the drain, circling the drain, circling the drain. I hear it slushing, slurping, and gurgling now. Free at last.

BTW. I think you mental health professionals as a group should spend more time studying individual human genomes. I am certain behaviors are genetically influenced way more than you can grasp. Biology, not psychology, is the key to mental problems. You can talk forever about decision-making, choices, and outcomes. I sense a person's genetic behavioral code has too much influence to be subdued or rehabbed completely using talk, conversation intervention, or therapy.

Call it biological fate if you like. Disagree? What about proclivities to be an alcoholic or diabetic or develop certain diseases?

Aren't people born gay? (I know. I've read the arguments on this. I know about the supposedly conflicting Xq28 chromosome and 2019 no single trait studies.) C'mon. I'm a math guy. I understand variables and stats. You can't have it both ways to fit the "discrete particular" (another Ross term signifying a specific instance which has little value in general application but gets the media's full attention) of the moment.

Finally. Your "helping profession" helps the most at fattening your own bank accounts. Big cars. Big houses. Huge turkeys at Thanksgiving.

That's it from Fleming. I am finished. Multi-dimensionally.

All those happy, loving couples enjoying anniversaries and Christmas Eve. Brother. Peace Out.

(Good luck to you, doc. If I can contact you from the other side, well, I will. I guess we are still friends. Please help Minerva if possible. She is wonderful. Thanks.)

~ Mr. Fleming at the Portal to Peace

Song of Myself, 32

"I think I could turn and live with animals, they are so placid and self-contain'd,
I stand and look at them long and long.

They do not sweat and whine about their condition,
They do not lie awake in the dark and weep for their sins,
They do not make me sick discussing their duty to God,
Not one is dissatisfied, not one is demented with the mania of owning things,
Not one kneels to another, nor to his kind that lived thousands of years ago,
Not one is respectable or unhappy over the whole earth."
~Walt Whitman

Appendix
(Essential for deepest understanding of Fleming's bizarre story)

"My Awakening: How I came to see the Text"

Originally published in *The Hobgoblin* - Online Journal 8/11/09
http://www.thehobgoblin.co.uk/journal/2009_thetext_aug09.htm

(Jeffrey Ross, who teaches English at a College in Arizona, explains how he learned to see the Text)

I have developed a frightening, yet powerful awareness. I now stand, mannequin-like, in the store window of life, grimly watching the Text driven crowds shuffle down the sidewalk, drifting into the distance, subsiding into the horizon. The Text was not in the beginning, but It came to be. Understanding the earliest incarnation of the Text is, well, difficult. Much like the Dao, the Text genesis is shrouded in mysterious and murky beginnings. Thick mists of time, space and conformity have glazed over its origins.

The Text has both oral and written traditions. Examples can be seen in the Horatio Alger rags-to-riches stories of the 19th century, and clearly heard in Sergeant Joe Friday's voice during 1960's episodes of *Dragnet*. Need a screen play to grasp the Text? Think, perhaps, of the late 1990's American movie *The Matrix*. Consider Jack Nicholson, angry and righteous, shouting, "You can't handle the truth" in *A Few Good Men*. We quiver and skulk, skeletal and shadowy forms, powerless to exert our humanity, or our human wisdom, before the power of the Text.

The Text booms from men as they speak on cell phones, confident and bellicose, making the next big business deal, checking flight reservations, wooing the partisans, impressing the trapped and yet eerily interested bystanders. The Text enjoys meetings and tabled decisions.

Disney Cruise ships, Mp3 players, LED TV's, Obama, Limbaugh, the Clintons, fish & chips, and Ralph Nader. The Text nurtures all. I hear the Text on *SpongeBob* and in the Provost's witticisms. The day care providers, the Harkins Movie ticket takers, the Fire Battalion Chief, the pool boy, the Democrat, the *Iron Chef*, Glen Beck, the *BBC News*, The Clash, the Foreign Legion. All pay homage and dues to the Text. The Text destroyed GM and Chrysler and had begun devouring my soul, too.

I see a Chinchilla, running on his wheel. I see the Text Energy at work. His glazed eyes are focused on some vectored point in the future, past associate professor status, the second home, perhaps happy withdrawals from a retirement account. He has read the latest leadership book, can say "absolutely" with clear diction in conversation, and can't wait to eat wings at Hooters during happy hour. "Whazzup," he grunts to the flip-flopped and T shirted Chinchilla, the one with the shaved head, in the cage next door.

The ceiling-smashing females at the workplace have (sadly) grasped the power of the Text and use the clipped speech forms common to the Text argot. They, too, have become slaves of the Text. Henry Ford once imagined the assembly line. Today, the Text mass produces Fords. Son of Man, I hear the Text groaning horribly. The Text has convinced us "chilling by the pool," burning fatty sausages over mesquite wood, quaffing imported beer, and Texting has some meaning beyond the commonplace.

The Text has given us Super Bowl commercials, Spring Break in Cancun, "Who Shot JR?," limos to the prom, the Euro, frequent flier miles, *American Idol*, *The Octomom*, March Madness, steroids, teeth whiteners, shared governance, and Hummers. What is the sum of all? The Text keeps a tally. The Text knows if you've been naughty or nice. The sum of all is zed. At the college, the Deans and Directors meet to celebrate the Text. The young Directors are giddy about the Text-given careers they have skewered. The aging Deans fearfully sense the Text has replaced the text they once knew and ostensibly understood and controlled. They are close to the truth. The Text is alpha; the old texts are beta. The Text has eaten and digested Shakespeare, Mencken, Hardy, sociology, feminism, and calculus. Today's menu includes Boethius, Hegel, Kant, Woolf, Sands, and Warhol.

The language of learning has been replaced by a droning buzz of the Text—the endless distillations of accountability, outcomes, market penetration, quality, training, partnering, customer service, succession planning, outreach, success vignettes, green buildings, delivery systems, upgrades, retention, kudos, and cosmos-stretching potlucks. (The Text loves potlucks, especially as an agenda item.) The Text has spread like May dandelions in the Colleges of Education. The Text demands accountability but will not be accountable. The Text is not the Immanent Will, or the Divine Afflatus, or some Spiritus Mundi. The Text has commoditized us all: our behavior, our dreams, our vacations, our teaching, our homes, our degrees, our philosophy, our God, our politics, our core sense of being.

The Text is not analog or kind. Children of The Text know nothing but the Text (the whole Text, ma'am), and appear from the digital Fields with glowing eyes and droid thoughts. To Challenge the Text means certain social annihilation—perhaps being sent adrift, out to sea, on a melting iceberg. Yea, but whosoever would be a man must reject the Text—and suffer.

One day, I started seeing the Text— oddly enough, while wearing 3D glasses. I was in The Big Film House, preparing to watch a comic, pleasant Pixar movie with my family. The Text became visible to me. Creepy as it sounds, I saw the Text in its munificent 3D glory up on the Blank Screen. Then I began to see my world much differently. I saw so many Chinchillas on treadmills. That moment, the switched flipped. That day, I started seeing the truth—the truth was not Disneyland, or CNN, or labor, or the college president's speeches, or career paths, or big talk, or granite counter tops, or inflated titles. Suddenly, iPods were plugging into students. The Vice Presidents were players in a morosely scripted drama produced by the Stimulus Package. That towering big-wheeled Lexus owned the Dean. Course Management Software became the medium and the message. Credit cards were sliding people through the slots.

Horrible, horrible, horrible.

I am no Rasputin, no Dostoevsky, no Gladstone, no blue-eyed Poe. Not even a sadly reflective Chekov. I take no medications and drink only moderately. Quietly, the truth came to me, an ancient truth from before the ice ages before the conifers. The truth whispered time and mortality. The truth glorified self-closure, dignity, life, social distance, honesty, freedom, and love. The truth is a tired mastodon breathing his last. I could no longer follow the Text. I felt sorry for the legions who embrace the Text. They seem childlike and trusting in their love of Text.

I now stand, mannequin-like, in the store window of my life, grimly watching the Text-driven crowds shuffle down the sidewalk, drifting into the distance, subsiding into the horizon.

I could not hurt them by publicly disavowing the Text.

Counseling and Care Clinic

Dr. Euyan Quanzo, M.D., PsyD
Psychotherapist
19 May 2021
John Fleming, Patient
Travel Trailer Park
Somewhere in Cococlippo County, AZ

Dear Mr. John Fleming,

As your assigned and designated Psychotherapist at the Cracking Sun Care and Counseling Center, I regret to inform you Cracking Sun can no longer offer you our services. The reasons for this board-recommended accommodation are many:

1) Your personal behavior within our facilities is unbecoming. A number of our staff, as well as many patients, have filed complaints regarding your inappropriate dress and behavior within the premises. "Shirtless and roaming" is how one RN described your dress.

2) Our staff has showed the *inability* to engage your attention,

through either medically-approved stimulation, conversation, and/or activities.

3) Your state funding for professional psychiatric care has been exhausted (in other words, you are broke). For these reasons, and many others, your affiliation with Cracking Sun and Counseling Care is terminated, effective immediately.

Sincerely,

Dr. Euyan Quanzo, M.D., PsyD
Psychotherapist and Chief of Staff
Cracking Sun Counseling and Care Clinic
Flagpole Arizona, 86000

Department of Arizona Pine Forests Enforcement Division

(This AZPFED directive was placed in a manila envelope and securely fastened to the back door of Fleming's travel/trailer camper unit. His whereabouts were unknown at that time. It is also unknown if Mr. Fleming has email or a designated USPS mailing address.)

January 7, 2022
Mr. John Fleming, Proprietor
Travel trailer/camper near 747 Forest Road
Happy Jack, Arizona

Dear Mr. Fleming,

This document serves as your final notice to remove your person, and your travel trailer/camper, from the premises located on the 747 Forest Road near Happy Jack, AZ.

1) The Department of Arizona Pine Forests has received numerous

complaints about a man living in this residence who walks about nude and uses the forest for "restroom-specific activities." Each of these behaviors are obvious misdemeanor offenses potentially resulting in jail sentences from 6 months to 8 years.

2) The designated occupancy time limit for camping in the specified forest zone is two weeks. Our records indicate you have been at your current location for four years, one month, and fifteen days. Because of your overstay in a time limit-specific camping area, you currently owe DAPF over $17,350 (Seventeen Thousand Three Hundred and Fifty Dollars) in fines and processing fees pursuant to AZ DAPF 666-1972. (In fact, one of our agents took a photo of your residence site on December 24, 2021. Your travel trailer/camper is pictured chained to a sign which contains information about camping time limits and possible fines.) If your travel trailer/camper is not moved by February 2, 2022, the trailer may be impounded at your expense.

3) You may pay your fines at the Cococlippo Courthouse in Flagpole AZ. Additionally, and to your benefit, we have convinced a federal judge to issue a 25-day leniency period for you. After February 2nd, 2022, a warrant will be issued for your arrest by US Marshals.

Have an enjoyable day,

Terry Galloway,

Chief Inspector
Department of Arizona Pine Forests Enforcement Division
Flagpole, AZ.

Department of Arizona Pine Forests Enforcement Division

February 25, 2022
Subject: Follow-up memo concerning Fleming Suicide Investigation
From: Terry Galloway, Chief Investigator, DAPFED
To: Vernon Boxwell, Chief of Police, Flagpole, AZ

We have emerging follow-up information for you RE: the Fleming investigation. As you know, a concerned citizen, known as Jane Doe, reported on February 14th she had not seen Fleming for several days. Our agency was in the process of evicting Fleming and his travel trailer/camper unit from the 747 Road site because of his overstay and violation of camping timeline policies.

DAPFED agents happened to be on site on February 2nd to serve a final eviction notice and/ or arrest Mr. Fleming. The door was wide open to his travel trailer/camper unit. Upon entering, our agents found several items of interest, including the suicide notes which have garnered so much public attention, a syringe, and an empty bottle of horse tranquilizer. Our agency now holds those items in a secured evidence locker.

Mr. John Fleming (living or dead) was not on the premise.

Debris, clothing (men's and women's) and papers were scattered everywhere. DAPFED Agent Bob Zontarg described the scene as "chaotic." **We also found the letter attached below**. No return address or envelope was discovered. The letter itself certainly has compelling language.
We have also placed the letter in our evidence locker.

That same concerned citizen, Jane Doe, called our office this morning, February 25, 2022, to say she was nearly certain she saw Fleming, and a middle-aged blonde female, at a campsite (with tent and portable shower) nearly four miles north of his travel trailer/camper unit.

The concerned citizen, Jane Doe, who was walking her dog, said she passed within fifteen yards of the tent campsite. The man she believes to be Fleming was strumming a guitar while singing something about "living in the archaic forest" and "I know you love me now" or "how do you like me now."

Doe said the woman was holding what appeared to be food items in her right hand—possibly peanuts or acorns. Several squirrels were present. Three rabbits watched from the shadows.

The small dog seated next to Fleming reportedly wagged his tail as the citizen and her own dog walked by, but she is certain the couple did not notice her presence.

Also, we have reports of an abandoned rental company SUV (with Florida license plates) near the sites mentioned above. DAPFED agents are currently investigating.

A significant problem exists with Jane Doe's report, however. She indicated, as she passed by, the couple and their small dog got up and turned to walk towards a brilliant **rainbow** which had formed in the forest. The National Weather Service did not report any precipitation in Cococlippo County on the date in question or the previous day. We are not sure if Ms. Doe was under the influence, hallucinating, or experiencing a possible paranormal situation. Certainly the "rainbow event" mentioned in her account seems hinky.

The investigation into the Fleming matter is ongoing. We are also conducting a nationwide search of missing persons data bases, police reports, and rental car records, to discover the woman's identity. At this time, Fleming is still officially missing.

To protect the integrity of the DAPFED investigation, we will not discuss any details with local media outlets. Please do not release the contents of this memo to the public. DAPFED considers Fleming to be a threat to himself and society

Department of Arizona Pine Forests Enforcement Division

February 25, 2022
Subject: Copy of letter found at abandoned Fleming Residence February 15
From: Terry Galloway, Chief Investigator, DAPFED
To: Vernon Boxwell, Chief of Police, Flagpole, AZ

January 16, 2021
Dear John,

Please stop sending me emails and presents. I vaguely remember meeting you at a mental health conference. I know we have exchanged friendly, interesting, and typically comforting emails and ideas since we belong to the same online self-help group. Certainly, we have struggled with many similar issues concerning love and family. Even so, please stop with the presents and cards. You are very thoughtful, but please stop.

The gifts are simply too much. I'm not sure how you found out about my birthday date. I suppose it is on the internet somewhere. Well, the flowers were genuinely nice, but the truck-delivered Shetland pony was a bit extravagant. Although ridiculously cute. Except the accompanying droppings my husband has to shovel. I have named the pony Rainbow Butterfly. My husband bought a nice prefab building to shelter Rainbow Butterfly.

Oh, I do appreciate the candy and poems. However, my husband was not pleased when the Over Eats guy delivered a seven-pound raspberry cheesecake with six of your poems attached to the package. A bit over the top, wouldn't you say?

BTW, I must admit your poems have a certain charismatic flair. Also, my husband was a bit perplexed by your gift of the complete stainless steel kitchen appliance suite on Valentine's ♥Day. (I sure appreciate the new refrigerator, though. So lovely. It even has that special dedicated wine dispenser. Mmm.)

Your assumption/hope I will leave my husband for an older man such as yourself is absurd. Don't you find it just a wee bit preposterous to think I would fall in love with some old white-haired bent-over former motorcycle-riding eccentric who lives in a leaky camper shell somewhere out in the Arizona forest? Hmm? My husband isn't very interesting, but he is certainly a good man and a decent provider. He looks better than you, too.

He does not really get poetry. He probably spends too much time playing video games and bowling down at the Maple Lanes with his best friend Luther, but whatever. Have I mentioned I am married and have a husband?

I don't even know where Happy Jack is located. I have no idea what airport I would fly to, or how I could rent a car or SUV. I think the biggest town near your place is Flagpole or something similar.

What I am saying is that this whole matter is insane. I am not leaving my fine three-story home sitting on a hectare of land, oh, and deserting my well-providing husband. Poetry, attention, and gifts are one thing, but your methods approach stalking. My husband mentioned a cease-and-desist order, but I said you are just being playful, and I would take care of things. I will, soon. He is a very secure and independent man. I hope this letter expresses my feelings. Thanks for everything, but isn't enough, enough? I mean really.

Even so, I do enjoy the forest. I love the birds, rabbits, and squirrels who live among the majestic pine trees. Things might be different if we had met or connected thirty years ago, but further correspondence isn't a good idea. For now.

Sincerely,
Y*** B****** M******

PS. Do you still have the same mean-spirited female roommate who beat you?

Flagpole AZ Police Department
We Strive for the Highest Level of Excellence—That is How We Roll

February 28, 2022
Subject: Letter received by Flagpole PD February 26
From: Vernon Boxwell, Chief of Police, Flagpole, AZ
To: Terry Galloway, Chief Investigator, DAPFED
(TG—we received this letter today. We're not sure what to make of it at this time. Who is the most delusional? Our follow up investigation continues. Thanks, Vern.)

2-26-2022
Dr. Chief of Police, Mr. Boxwell,

    My name is Thomas Braddock, but folks call me Tom, and I am hoping you can help me. I would come talk to you in person, but I live in Florida, and Arizona is almost all the way across the country.

    My wife Yolanda ('Landa for short) has bipolar disorder, the really bad kind which causes hallucinations and things, just like her dad's got. Back when we were dating, she was Minerva then but hated her name. She had her name changed when we got married. Her family's head shrinker, Dr. Quanzo, told me she had symptoms since she was a teenager, and to always be mindful of her meds. She does really good when she's on them, but when she goes off, that's when things get, well, interesting, because she can't always tell the difference between her delusions and reality. Just like her dad.

    Well, I am ashamed to say I might have a tiny part to play in all this mess, but I swear I never meant for it to get out of hand. When she first started getting flowers and little gifts from him, it was no big deal. Then, the gifts started getting bigger and, well, he's loaded you know, and I liked the things he was sending, so I told her to play along with it. (Secretly I'd been hoping for a motorcycle, but I have to admit the new kitchen appliances were quite an upgrade for us.)

I was going to put a stop to things when he sent the pony, though. I mean, who sends a grown woman a pony for her birthday? Then, I noticed 'Landa was so happy, and said she'd wanted one since she was a little girl, so how could I make her send it back? Besides, HOW do you send a pony back? So, I just kept going along, even though I knew it wasn't right. Shoot, just because John Fleming is confused and thinks his daughter is a B movie starlet who might run away with him doesn't mean he can't send her nice things, right?

You see 'Landa's old man Fleming has been in and out of the hospital a lot—three weeks here, two months there. He would always tell stories. Sometimes they were about a woman he met and fell in love with at a conference, other times about a psychotherapist he "lived with" and who beat him. As far as I know, John didn't live with anyone. The psychotherapist was probably just a fellow shut-in he picked fights with at the mental hospital, and the "woman," I am now realizing, was 'Landa who flew to see him once and took him flowers to thank him for some nice thing he'd sent.

Now I know what you are thinking, and you're right. I am a terrible man for letting my father-in-law believe his daughter (my wife) is really his secret crush, and then go on to fake his own suicide to he can be with her.

Things get a little worse, I suppose, when I tell you at some point I knew 'Landa was living his delusion, too. At Thanksgiving last year, she kept giggling and whispering to her cousins about her "secret admirer" (dad). She told them she wanted to live with him in the forest. At the time it confused me, so I tried not to think about it (plus Christmas was coming and I was still hoping for a motorcycle).

When I confronted her about old Fleming in January, she denied anything crazy was about to happen, and even wrote a stop-sending-me-stuff letter to him. When she didn't come home from the grocery store a few weeks ago, though, that's when I figured out the letter was probably a fake, just meant to get me off the trail.

I know this looks pretty bad, but it is still mostly under control, as long as we act fast, before anything "improper" happens. 'Landa is not usually sneaky, and John's not highly creative. Attached is a map of the Arizona Pine Forest, with a big "X" on it. I found this map taped to the back of the nice stove he sent us.

I tried contacting Dr. Quanzo for help in getting 'Landa back home, but he said he's washed his hands of this family, so I'm reaching out to you. If you all could just go get her and send her back home, I'd sure appreciate it.

Sincerely and a little apologetically,
Tom Braddock

P.S. I know this might be a big ask, but if you could, please don't mention the whole "he's your dad/she's your daughter" thing. Her birthday is five months away, and we could really use a new bedroom set. Plus, there's still always hope for my motorcycle.

If you or someone you know may be considering suicide, contact the **National Suicide Prevention Lifeline** at 1-800-273-8255 (En Español: 1-888-628-9454; Deaf and Hard of Hearing: 1-800-799-4889) or the <u>Crisis Text Line</u> by texting HOME to 741741.

Dr. Hill's Poet

A sixty-three-year-old literature professor and his forty-one-year-old student fall in love despite criticism (and moral judgement) from his university, the community, and their circle of friends. Sam and Cassie's commitment to each other, and their love of poetry, sustains the relationship and brings them new awareness about the connections between art and life. Brought together by a powerful destiny, their romance is also nurtured by the world of nature and honest and direct communication. *Dr. Hill's Poet* is richly descriptive of the Platte River Valley in central Nebraska. This pleasant and fast-moving story contains textual elements common to traditional fiction, poetry, and the screen play genre.

At the Community College: Smiles and Reflections

Community colleges provide valuable learning experiences for millions of Americans. But they are not mini-universities or dedicated trade schools—they offer a unique higher-ed pathway which is often misunderstood and sometimes under-appreciated. This book provides a behind-the-scenes look at daily community college life—from student, administrative, board, and faculty perspectives! You will learn (or recognize) a great deal about daily community college machinations and the "characters" who are hard at work to make the community college journey "sustainable." Both humorous and revealing, the engaged reader will come away with a new appreciation for the American Community College Event!

Silent Sonora

Silent Sonora details the life of a heroic young girl, Lillian Carroll, whose family resides in two tents during the 1920's and 1930's. Set in depression-era Scottsdale Arizona, this true story reveals Lillian's daily life experiences, the family's struggles, and her quest for a better life through education. Lillian tells readers directly about tent life, the local "emerging" Arizona communities, and the ongoing hardships she and her family confront. Both of Lillian's parents are deaf—her father works in the local agricultural industry, while her strong-willed mother endeavors to make the best home she can for her children. Lillian admits that "life was tough," but assures us she and her family had good times, too. Ultimately, Lillian's desire for a better education helps her situation—her love of family and strong faith give her the support she needs to finally gain independence.

College Leadership Crisis: The Philip Dolly Affair

A Crisis in Community College Leadership: The Phillip Dolly Affair is literary in development but grounded in "chaotic" community college daily experience. The novel is comic, satiric, quasi-politically correct, edgy, and richly descriptive of community college life, leadership foibles, and cultural themes. This hyperbolic text is entertaining, edifying, and fun. Little community college fiction—comic or otherwise—exists—the authors are fearless in their humorous—and sometimes biting—analysis of community college culture....

The "stereotype-busting" authors reacquaint readers with the [faded] ideals of the 1960's social renaissance.

While community colleges are currently receiving heightened attention, this novel provides a behind-the-scenes analysis of many "whispered truths," those simmering but unspoken workplace issues, behaviors, and machinations nearly every worker [Everyman] in America will recognize.

Love in the RV Park: A Romance for Men

This quirky and fast moving romance revolves around passionate lovers in tangled and mostly unfulfilling relationships. The tale is complete with hot housewives, rock musicians, exotic dancers, motorcycles, steamy nail polish-melting love scenes, hard drinking college professors, hybrid alien children, a romantic bug exterminator, girl fights, a New Year's Eve brawl, religious zealotry, prophecies (The Temple of Just DOET)—and more. Ultimately, Love in the RV Park is about the male perception (misperception?) of the female psyche—and the novel attempts to answer an age-old question: What do women want? Laugh or cry—you'll come away enlightened after reading this zany romance.

The Auroran: Cold Front Redemption

August Nightingale, in late middle age, has had little success with relationships-- and not much meaningful satisfaction in the world of work. Abruptly deciding to "leave it all behind," he embarks on a snowy road trip to visit Civil War battlefields in Pennsylvania. His journey becomes one of self-realization. A mishap on the highway, the kindness of his beautiful neighbor Sarah (who helps him to convalesce), and the friendly people of Aurora change his life and his heart. This mature romance novel shows that it is never too late to find happiness, to experience meaningful love, when souls are honest and open to the truths of human experience.

1040 Taxes Could be Replaced by One-Cent Fees!

1040 culture—like it or not—exists because the United States government taxes personal income to raise trillions to fund the federal treasury. This amount will undoubtedly increase in the future—but so will American commerce and the GDP. The focus of this book will be how we can raise 3.5 or 5.0 or 6 trillion dollars efficiently and accurately while eliminating the unwieldy 1040 tax return process. The TFP plan, basically, is to "automatically" assess a 1 cent fee (.01 dollar) on all trackable transactions in the US (or related international transactions using American financial institutions). Say good bye to tax preparation, deductions, refunds, credits—this will be a pay-as-you-go system. Tax audits and tax-related stress will become history.

About the Author

Jeffrey Ross, who resides in Arizona, is a writer, musician, and former full-time community college teacher. He has had four "Views" pieces published on *InsidehigherEd.com,* has authored and co-authored several national and international op-ed articles on community college identity, purpose, and culture, and has published numerous parody poems and articles.

Ross co-authored the comic and critically acclaimed campus novel *College Leadership Crisis: The Philip Dolly Affair* (Rogue Phoenix Press, 2011). He also authored the romance parody *Love in the RV Park: A Romance for Men* (Rogue Phoenix Press, 2013), the nonfiction life history about 1920s life in Scottsdale, Arizona *Silent Sonora* (Rogue Phoenix Press 2015), a mature romance *The Auroran: Cold Front Redemption* (Rogue Phoenix Press 2016), and the researched policy proposal *1040 Taxes Could be Replaced by One-Cent Fees!* (Rogue Phoenix Press 2018).

Many readers have enjoyed his analysis of the community college experience, *At the Community College: Smiles and Reflections* (Rogue Phoenix Press, 2019). Ross, along with co-authors Brian Franzen and Michael Newlun, wrote the interesting travel book *Southwest by Two Stroke: Riding 350 Yamahas to California*, which describes their 1973 motorcycle ride from Nebraska to California and back (Rogue Phoenix Press, 2019). Ross recently wrote a "sweet romance" with both prose and poetry about a professor and his student who fall in love, *Dr. Hill's Poet* (Rogue Phoenix press, 2021). Ross co-authored the epic continent-crossing motorcycle travel book *Riding 500cc Two-Strokes to Canada from Arizona in 1972 and other Motorcycle Adventures* with Jim Balding (Rogue Phoenix Press, 2021). Ross also co-authored *Eastbound to Life: Riding 350cc Two-Strokes from Nebraska to Boston in 1974 And Other Coming-of-Age Stories* (Rogue Phoenix Press, 2022) with Brian Franzen.

www.ingramcontent.com/pod-product-compliance
Lightning Source LLC
Chambersburg PA
CBHW070641130626
46555CB00006B/2646

* 9 7 8 1 6 2 4 2 0 7 2 6 6 *